Catch Me If You Can!

W9-CNU-766

Bernard Most

Green Light Readers
Harcourt, Inc.
Orlando   Austin   New York   San Diego   London

He was the biggest dinosaur of them all.
The other dinosaurs were afraid of him.

When the biggest dinosaur went by,
the other dinosaurs quickly hid.

They were afraid of his great big tail.

They were afraid of his great big claws.

They were afraid of his great big feet.

But most of all, they were afraid of
his great big teeth.

One little dinosaur wasn't afraid.
She didn't run. She didn't hide.

"Catch me if you can!" she called
to the biggest dinosaur.

"I'm not afraid of your great big tail.

Catch me if you can!"

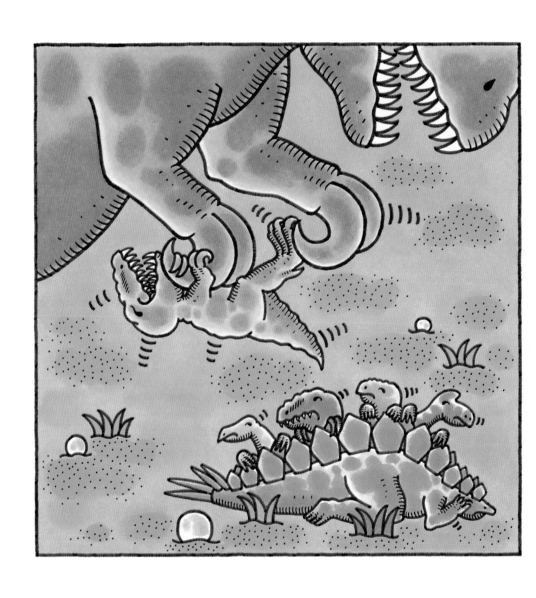

"I'm not afraid of your great big claws.

Catch me if you can!"

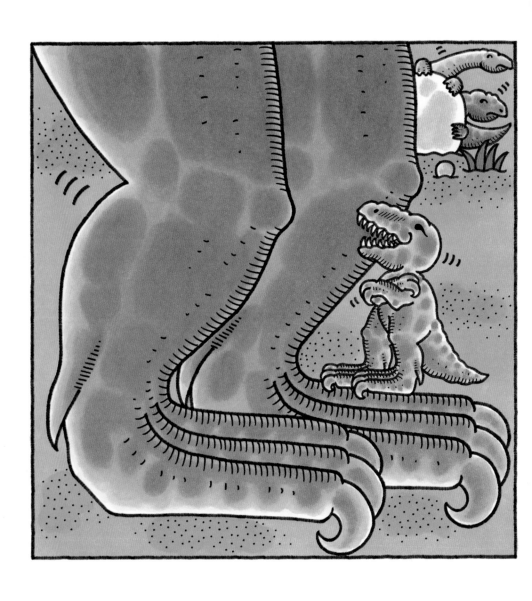

"I'm not afraid of your great big feet.

Catch me if you can!"

"And most of all, I'm not afraid of your great big teeth."

"I can catch you!" said the biggest dinosaur.
And he grabbed the little dinosaur.

But she only got a big hug.
"I love you very much, Grandpa!"
said the little dinosaur.

"And I love you, too!"
said the biggest dinosaur of them all.

DINOSAUR TAG

Play a dinosaur game with a
big group of friends.

1 Line up. Put your hands on the next person's shoulders.

2 The first person 😊 is the head. The last person 😊 is the tail.

3 The head 🦎 tries to catch the tail. 🦎

When the head catches the tail, play again!

Meet the Author-Illustrator

Bernard Most knew he wanted to be an artist even before he went to kindergarten. Later, he went to art school and became an artist. He saw some books by Leo Lionni and liked them so much that he started to write his own books for children.

Bernard Most works hard on his books. He sent out one book forty-two times before it was published! He didn't give up. He knew how important it is to believe in yourself and to keep trying.

Bernard Most